This Walker book
belongs to:

_____

_____

Penguin

Polly Dunbar

WALKER BOOKS
AND SUBSIDIARIES

LONDON · BOSTON · SYDNEY · AUCKLAND

Ben ripped open his present.

Inside was a penguin.

"Hello, Penguin!" said Ben.

"What shall we play?" said Ben.

Penguin said nothing.

"Can't you talk?" said Ben.

Penguin said nothing.

Ben tickled Penguin.

Penguin didn't laugh.

Ben pulled his funniest face
for Penguin.

Penguin didn't laugh.

Ben put on a happy hat

and sang a silly song

and did a dizzy dance.

Penguin said nothing.

"Will you talk to me if I stand on
my head?" said Ben.

Penguin didn't say a word.

So Ben prodded Penguin

and blew a raspberry at Penguin.

Penguin said nothing.

Ben made fun of Penguin

and imitated Penguin.

Penguin said nothing.

Ben ignored Penguin.

Penguin ignored Ben.

So Ben fired Penguin into outer space ...

Penguin came back to Earth without a word.

Ben tried to feed Penguin
to a passing lion.

Penguin said nothing.

Lion didn't want to eat Penguin.

Ben got upset.

Penguin said nothing.

Lion ate Ber

or being too noisy.

Penguin bit Lion
very hard
on the nose.

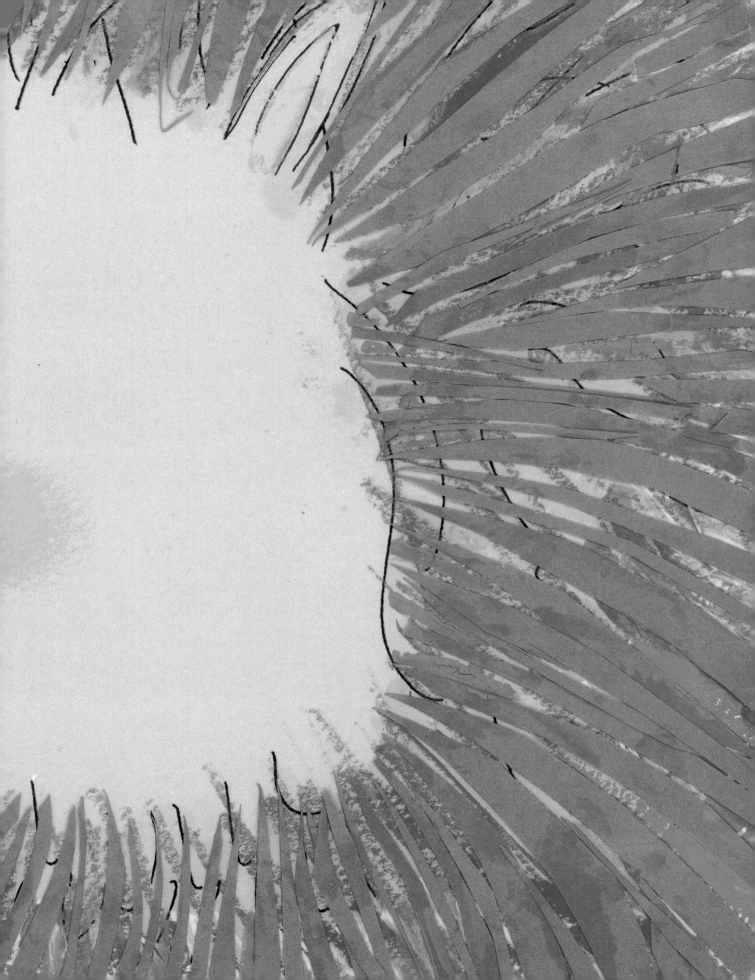

said Lion.

said Ben.

And Penguin said ...

everything!

Polly Dunbar

Since publishing her first book at just sixteen years of age, Polly Dunbar has become one of today's most exciting young author-illustrators. Full of warmth and wit, her enchanting books have captivated children around the world.

Polly is also part-founder of the touring puppet company Long Nose Puppets, which produced a hugely successful adaptation of her book **Shoe Baby**.

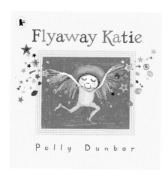

ISBN 978-1-84428-517-4

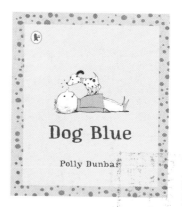

ISBN 978-1-84428-514-3

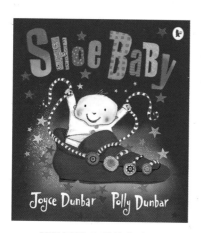

ISBN 978-1-4063-0161-8

ISBN 978-1-4063-2711-3

Available from all good booksellers

www.walker.co.uk